Max's Dinosaur Feet!

For my dearest daughters
Alessia and Elina.
~ L S

For James and Beth
With special thanks to my family.
~ P P

First published in the UK in 2019
This edition printed 2019
by New Frontier Publishing Europe Ltd
Uncommon, 126 New King's Road, Fulham, London, SW6 4LZ
www.newfrontierpublishing.co.uk

ISBN: 978-1-912858-19-4

Text copyright © 2019 Lana Spasevski
Illustrations copyright © 2019 Penelope Pratley
The rights of Lana Spasevski to be identified as the author and
Penelope Pratley to be identified as the illustrator of this work have been asserted.

A CIP catalogue record for this book
is available from the British Library.

Designed by Verity Clark

Printed in China
10 9 8 7 6 5 4 3 2

Max's Dinosaur Feet!

Lana Spasevski

Penelope Pratley

Max has **dinosaur** feet.

SToMp!

StaMp!

SMAsh!

'Dinosaur stampede!' roars Max.

'Shhh, you'll wake
Molly,' whispers Mum.
'Walk softly, Dinosaur
Max,' she adds.

Max looks at his dinosaur
feet. 'How?' he asks.

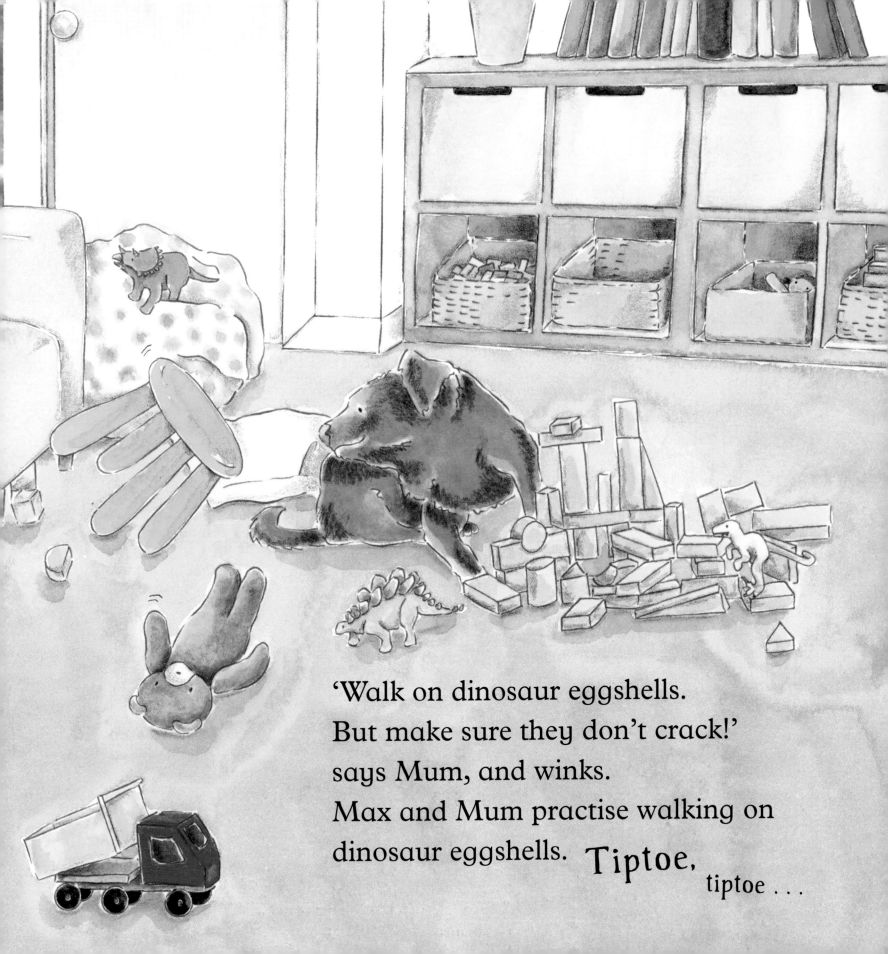

'Walk on dinosaur eggshells.
But make sure they don't crack!'
says Mum, and winks.
Max and Mum practise walking on
dinosaur eggshells. Tiptoe,
tiptoe . . .

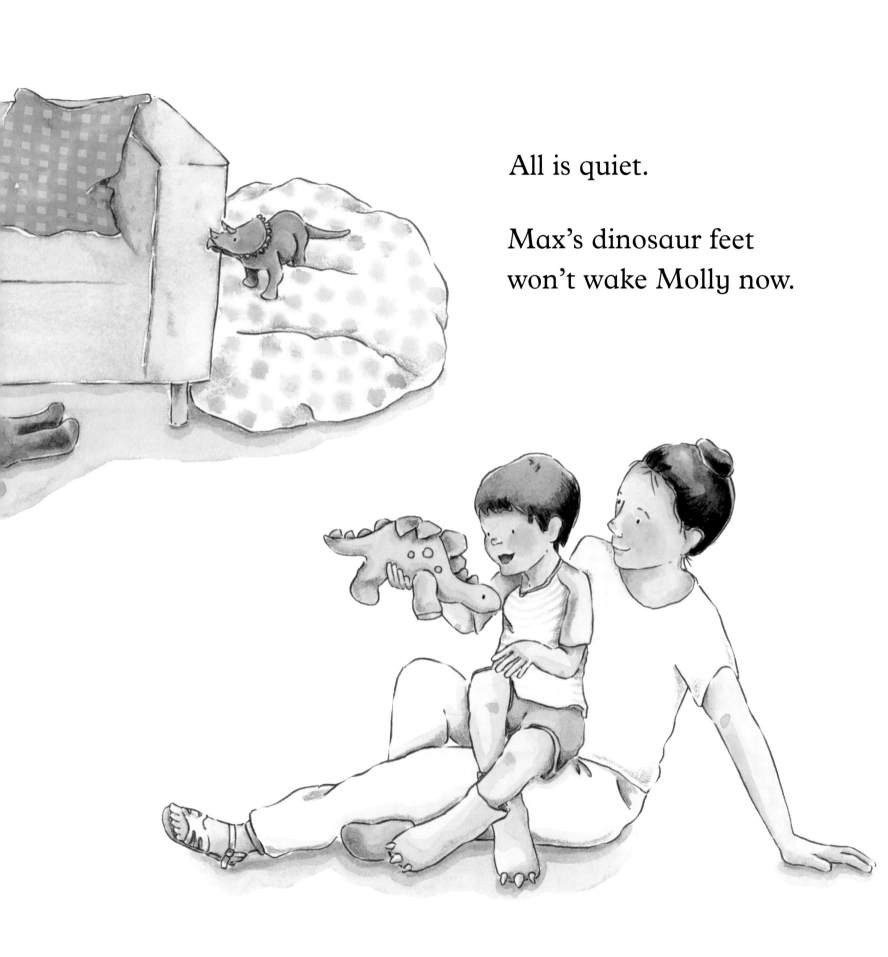

All is quiet.

Max's dinosaur feet
won't wake Molly now.

But Dad's happy summer feet will.

Drip!

Slip!

Flip!

'Shhh, you'll wake Molly,' hushes Max.

'Follow us, Dad.
We'll show you how
to walk on dinosaur
eggshells.'

Tiptoe,

tiptoe . . .

All is quiet again.

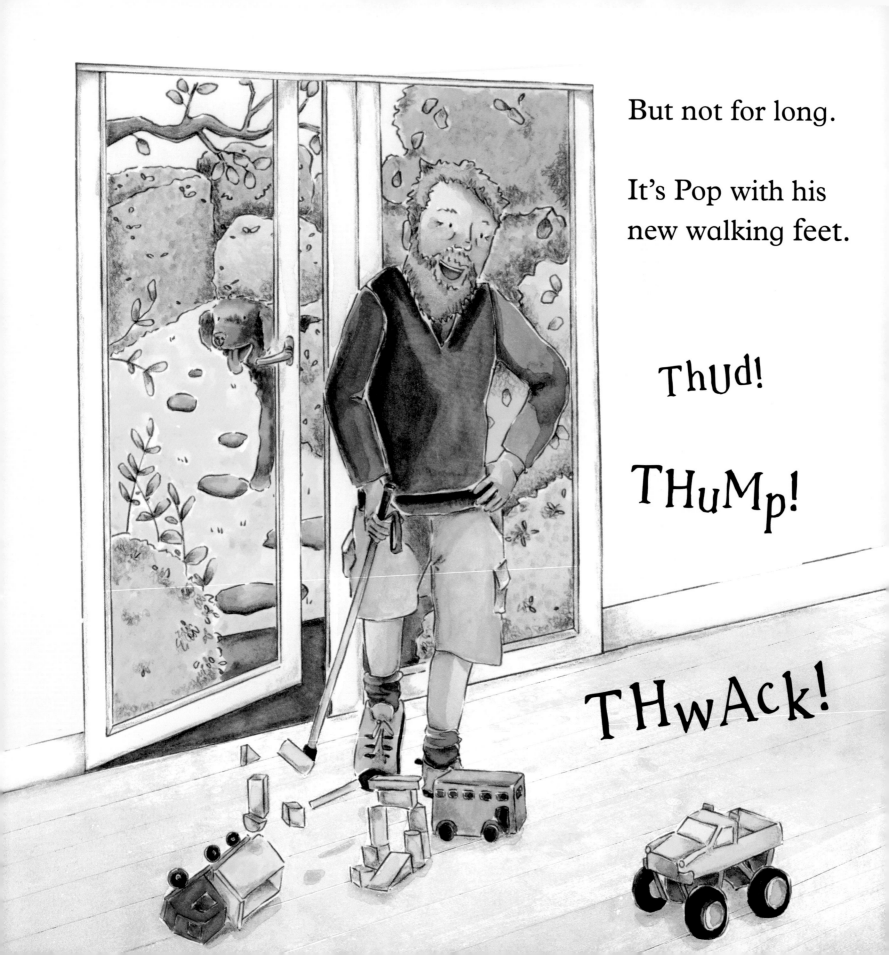

But not for long.

It's Pop with his
new walking feet.

ThUd!

THuMp!

THwAck!

'Shhh, you'll wake
Molly!' squeals Max.

'Follow us, Pop. We'll show you how to walk on dinosaur eggshells.'

Tiptoe,

tiptoe . . .

All is quiet again.

But then Merida prances in
with her dazzling dancing feet.

SwiSh!

SwOOsh!

SwAy!

'Shhh, you'll wake
Molly!' cries Max.

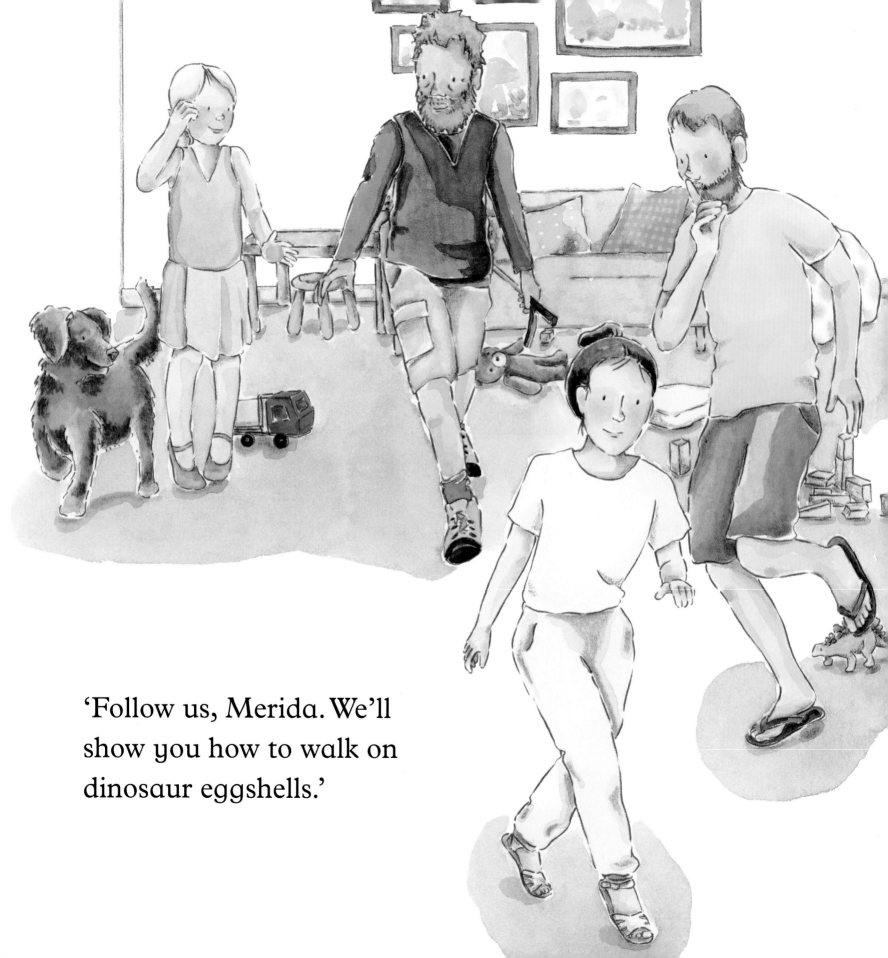

'Follow us, Merida. We'll show you how to walk on dinosaur eggshells.'

Tiptoe,

tiptoe . . .

Finally, all is quiet.

But then Rufus charges in.
He has a wrinkly wet nose
that just loves feet!

Sniff!

'WAAAHHHH!'

There is Molly.
She has teeny tiny
baby feet.

Tip,

tap,

twinkle.

'I'm sorry our noisy feet woke you, Dinosaur Molly,' says Max.

'Close your eyes. I'll tell you a story,' he whispers.

'Once upon a time,
there were five little dinosaurs.

This little dinosaur went to the forest,
This little dinosaur stayed home.
This little dinosaur had roasted leaves for dinner,
And this little dinosaur had none.'

'This little dinosaur got very, very sleepy and yawned all the way home.'

Tiptoe,

tiptoe . . .

All is quiet again.

For now . . .